#5 ±28

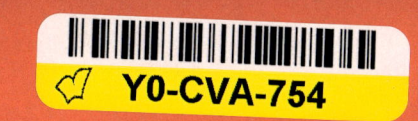

I CAN READ ABOUT

RACING CARS

Written by C. J. Naden
Illustrated by Herb Mott

Troll Associates

Copyright ©1979 by Troll Associates
All rights reserved. No part of this book may be used or reproduced
in any manner whatsoever without written permission from the publisher.
Printed in the United States of America. Troll Associates, Mahwah, N.J.
Library of Congress Catalog Card Number: 78-74658
ISBN 0-89375-216-9

These words are the start of one of the world's most exciting races—the Indianapolis 500. It is the best-known automobile race in the United States. Drivers from many countries race in the Indianapolis 500. If you win, you know you're good. And the world knows it, too!

The Indianapolis 500 is only one of many races. There are stock car races and sports car races. There are short races and long races, road races and track races. Anyone who enters any race wants the same thing—to be the *fastest!* Speed is what racing is all about.

Modern Indianapolis winners may average 170 miles, or 274 kilometers, an hour.

There are two main kinds of racing—*road racing* and *track racing*.

Many road races are held on public roads. They have lots of turns, and sometimes they are hilly. Some races run right through the center of a town.

ZOOM...

It is exciting to watch one car try to pass another car on a curve in a road race.

Road racing is very popular in Europe. But there are road races in the United States and Canada, too.

The most famous road races are called Grand Prix (Grahn Pree) Races. In a little country in Europe, there is a big race. In the Monaco Grand Prix, the world's best drivers speed their cars through twisting streets.

The United States has a big Grand Prix, too. It is held in the village of Watkins Glen, New York.

Grand Prix automobiles have a special name—Formula One cars. They are the stars of auto racing. Formula One cars are beautiful machines.

They are brightly colored, with fat rubber tires. These sports cars are built very low to the ground. They have one seat and no fenders.

There's plenty of excitement on Grand Prix racing day. All the best drivers are there. Who will be the winner?

The winning driver must be first over the finish line after a certain number of runs, or laps around the course. At Watkins Glen, the course is over three miles long. The cars must race around it 59 times.

There are other road races for sports cars.

Big, high-speed sports racers run in the Canadian-American (Can-Am, for short) Challenge Cup. These racing cars are called Can-Am cars.

Some sports racers look very much like regular sports cars. They have two seats and fenders. But their engines are very powerful. The big sports car race held in Daytona Beach, Florida lasts for 24 hours!

Small, closed cars, called sedans, enter Trans-American (Trans-Am, for short) road races. In these races, it is the winning type of car, not the winning driver, that is named the champ!

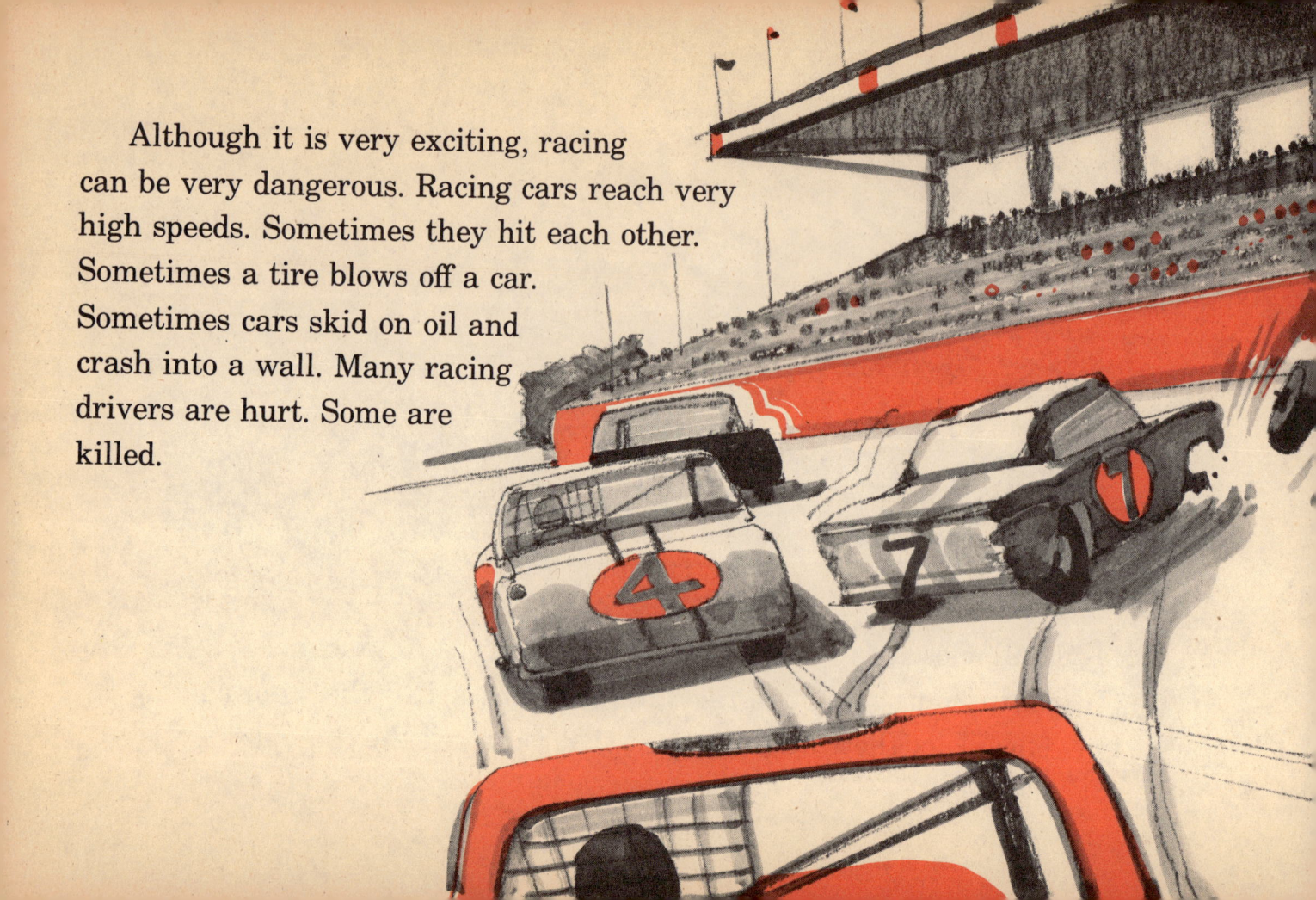

Although it is very exciting, racing can be very dangerous. Racing cars reach very high speeds. Sometimes they hit each other. Sometimes a tire blows off a car. Sometimes cars skid on oil and crash into a wall. Many racing drivers are hurt. Some are killed.

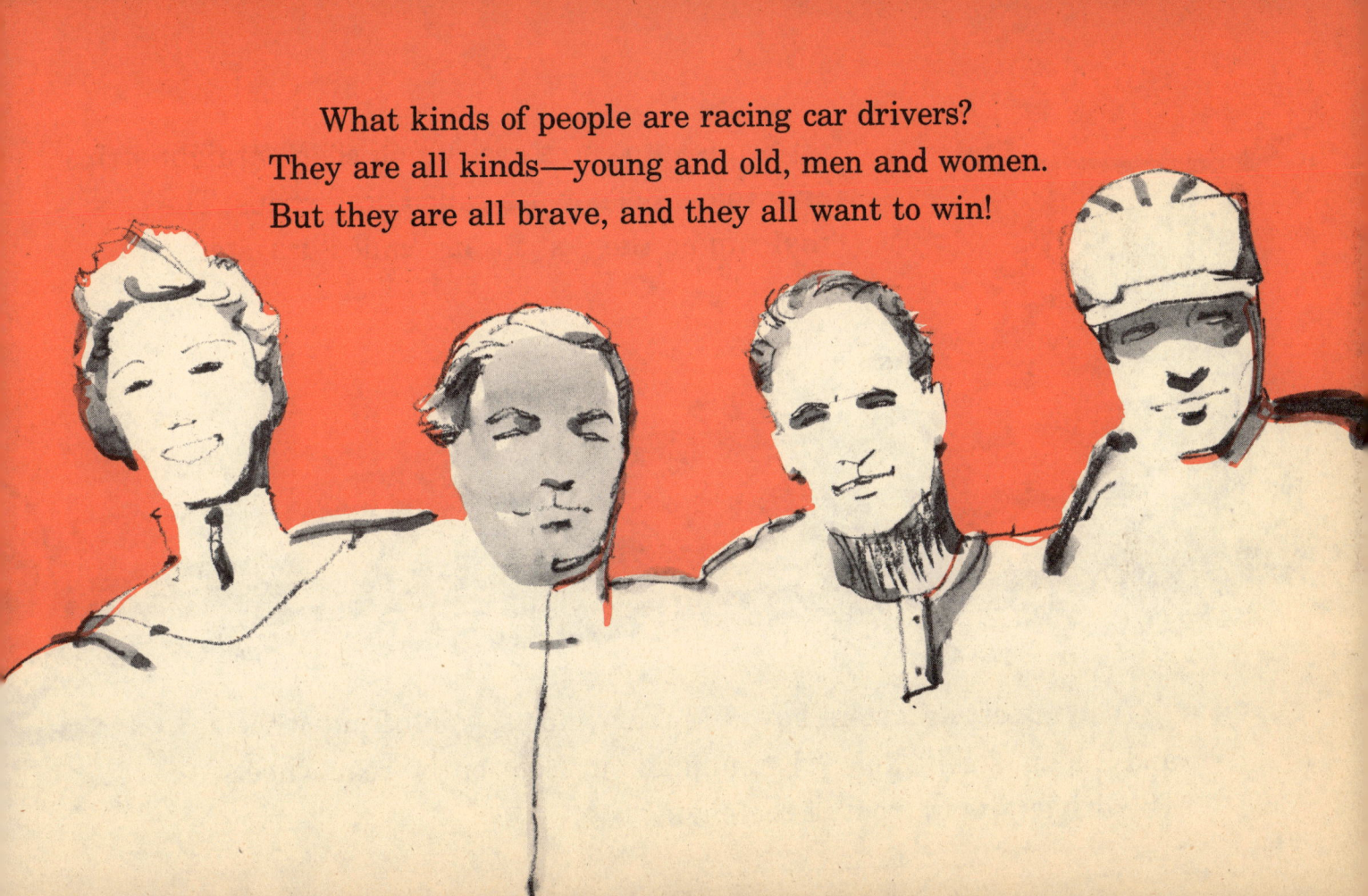

What kinds of people are racing car drivers?
They are all kinds—young and old, men and women.
But they are all brave, and they all want to win!

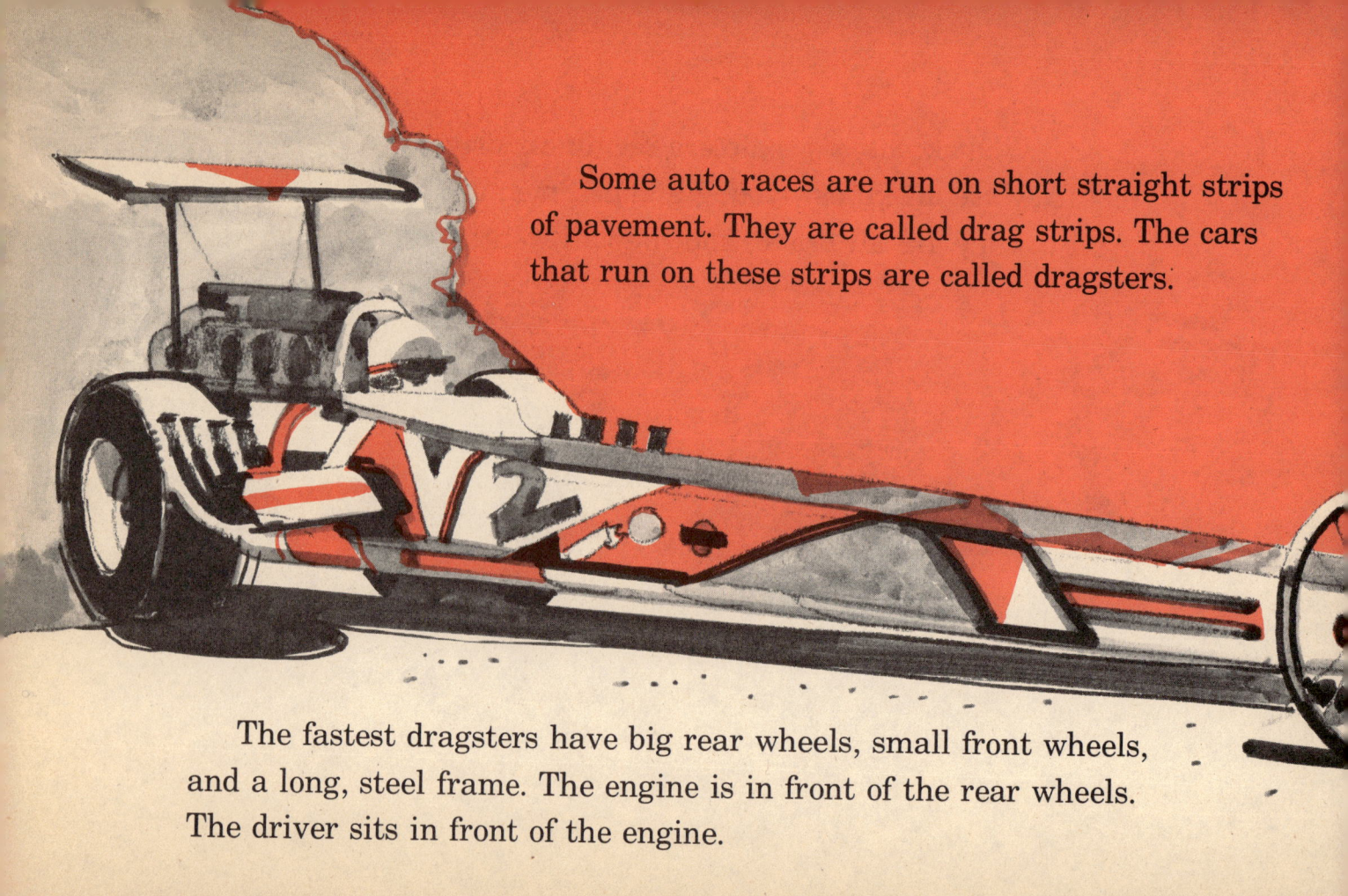

Some auto races are run on short straight strips of pavement. They are called drag strips. The cars that run on these strips are called dragsters.

The fastest dragsters have big rear wheels, small front wheels, and a long, steel frame. The engine is in front of the rear wheels. The driver sits in front of the engine.

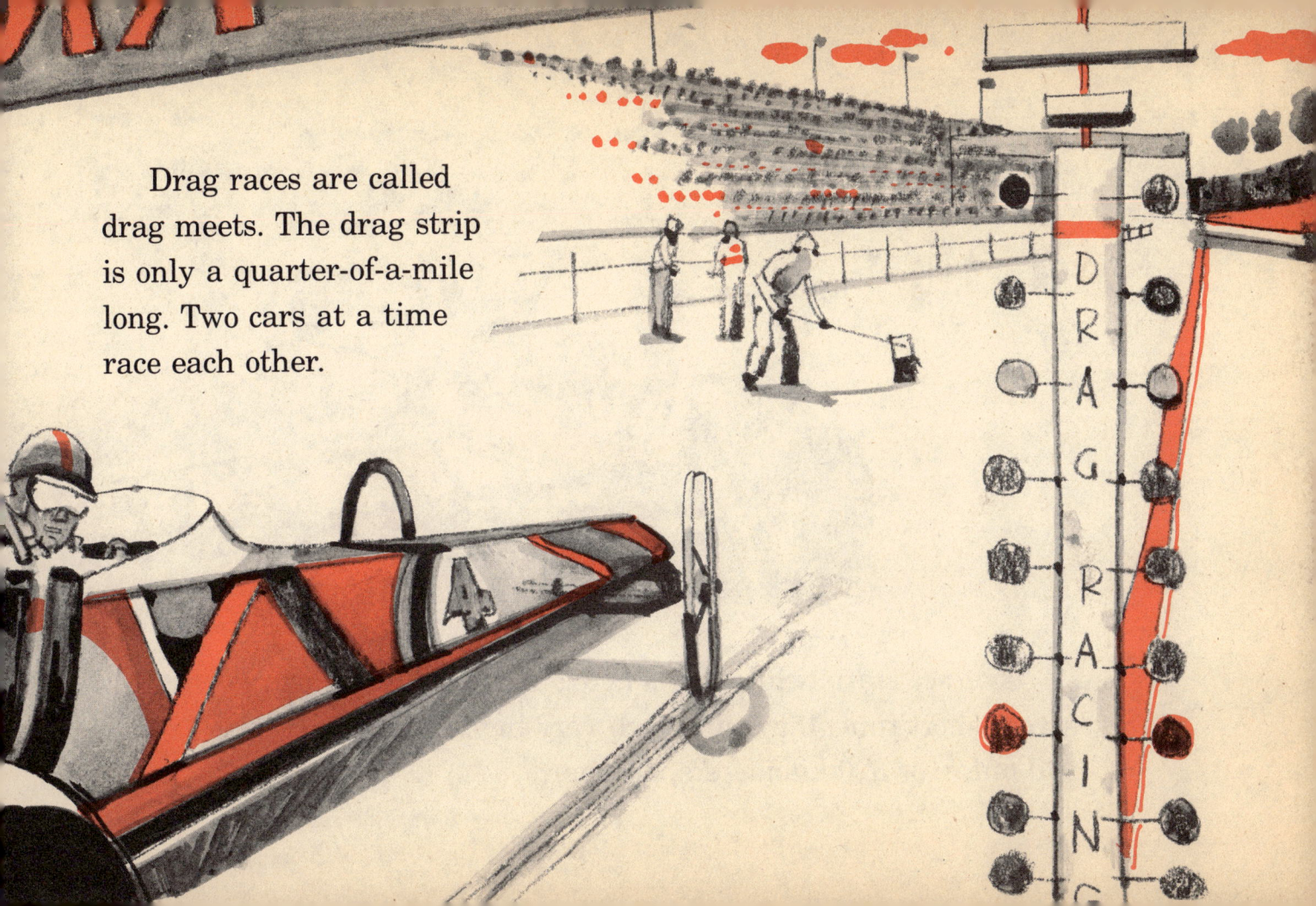

Drag races are called drag meets. The drag strip is only a quarter-of-a-mile long. Two cars at a time race each other.

The race starts while the cars are standing still. But in a very short time, they can reach very high speeds—perhaps 200-miles, or 320-kilometers, an hour.

Dragsters move too fast to stop like normal cars.

Most of them have to open up a parachute behind the car to stop it.

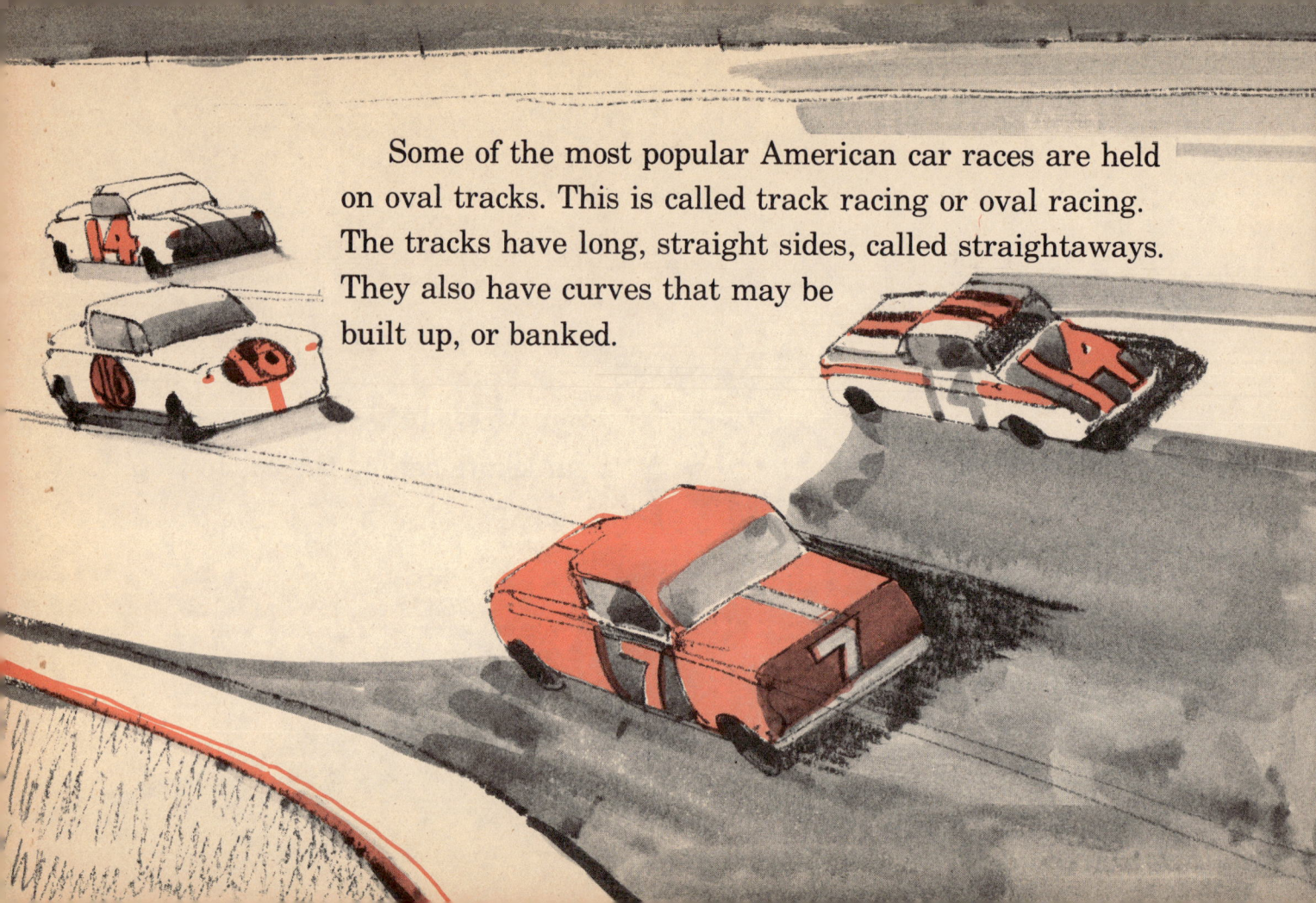

Some of the most popular American car races are held on oval tracks. This is called track racing or oval racing. The tracks have long, straight sides, called straightaways. They also have curves that may be built up, or banked.

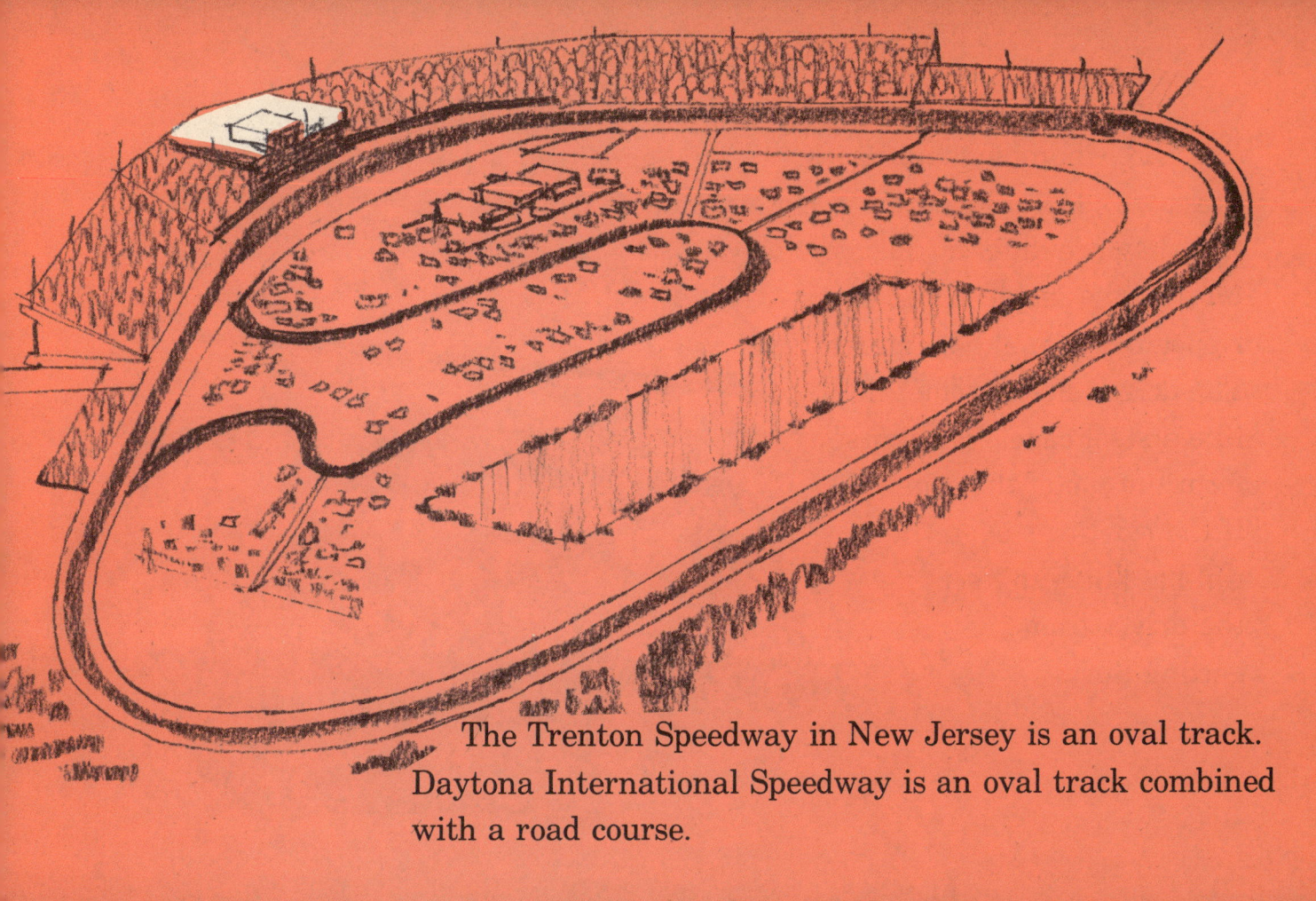

The Trenton Speedway in New Jersey is an oval track. Daytona International Speedway is an oval track combined with a road course.

There are two main types of track races—Stock Car Races and U.S. Championship Races.
Stock cars look like ordinary closed cars. But they are different in many ways. Most of the inside of the car is ripped out to make it lighter. The driver sits in something like a steel cage. "Roll bars" form the top of the cage. If the car turns over, the roll bars help to keep the driver from getting hurt.

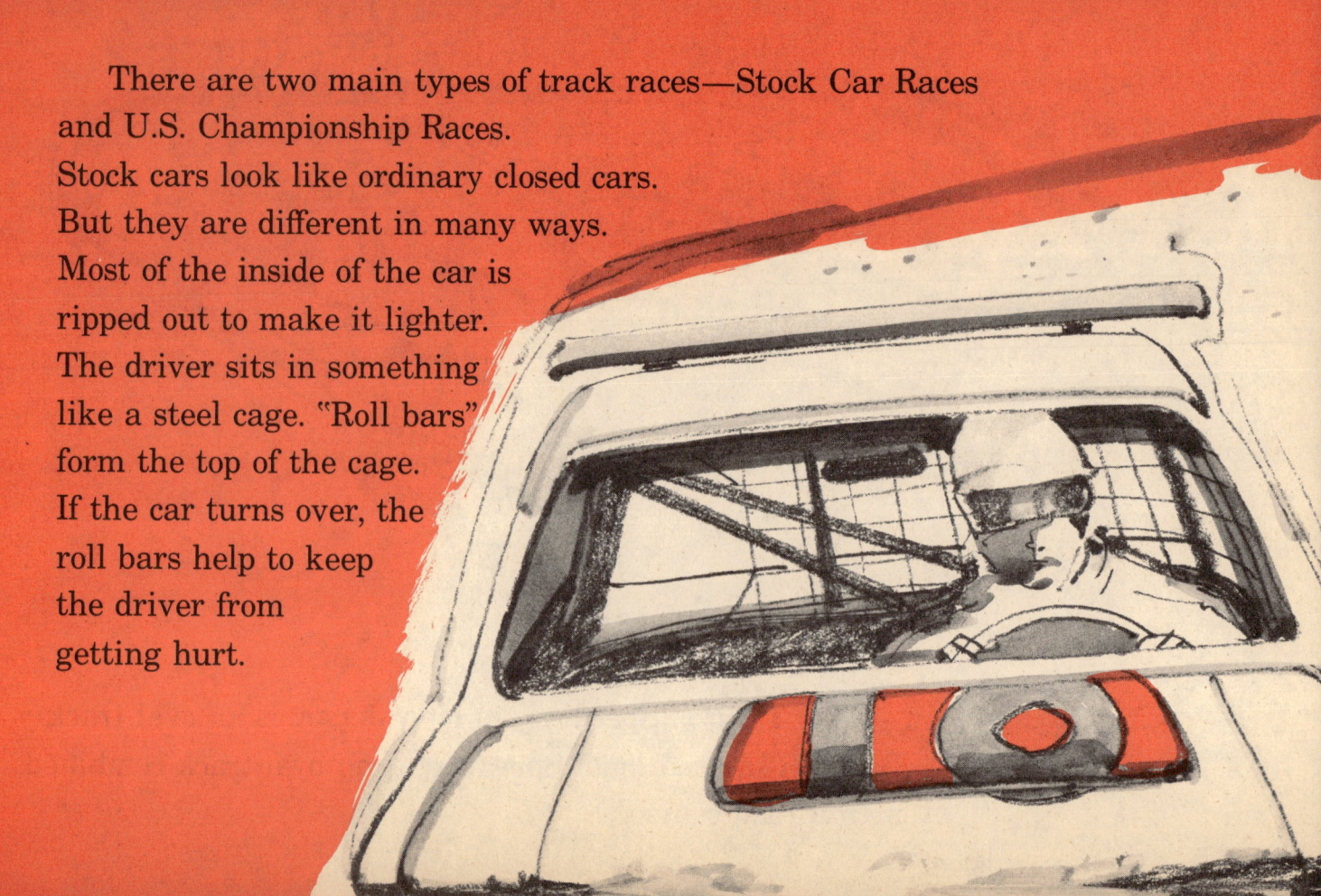

A stock car can look like an old wreck. Or it could be a brand new model. Newer stock cars run in the Grand National Championship Races. These races can be as long as 600 miles, or 960 kilometers.

There are about twenty U.S. Championship Races each year. They are called the Championship Trail. Winners and runners-up get points at the end of each Championship Trail Race.

The driver with the most points in a year is the U.S. Champion.

Most Championship Races are track races. But one of the races runs right up Pikes Peak in the Rocky Mountains of Colorado.

The cars that enter U.S. Championship Races are called Championship cars or Indy (for Indianapolis) cars. They are much like Grand Prix cars. They are beautiful, low and shining. Like Grand Prix cars, an Indy car is also very fast and can cost a great deal of money.

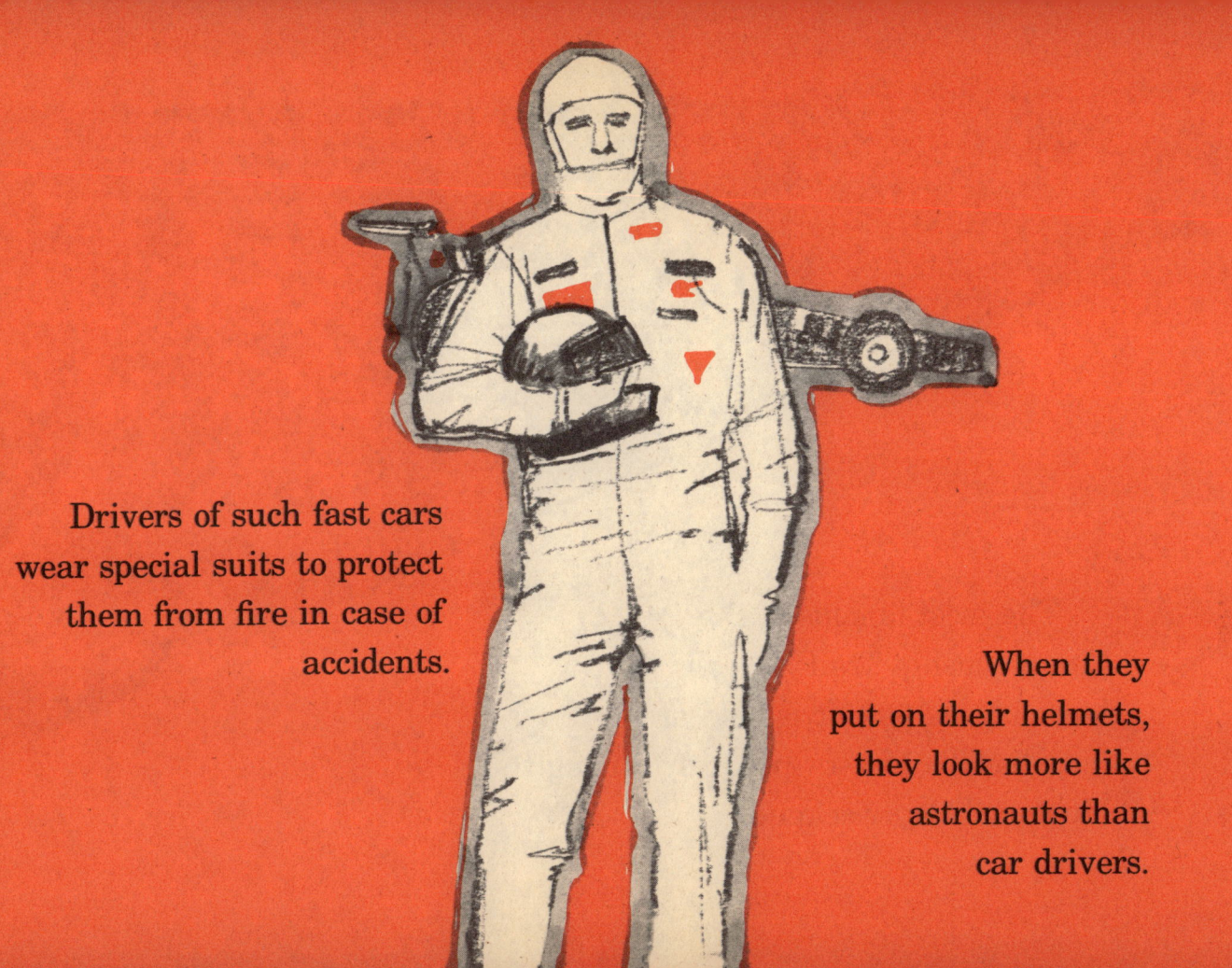

Drivers of such fast cars wear special suits to protect them from fire in case of accidents.

When they put on their helmets, they look more like astronauts than car drivers.

The most famous of the Championship Trail Races is the Indianapolis 500. It is held at the Indianapolis Motor Speedway during the Memorial Day weekend.

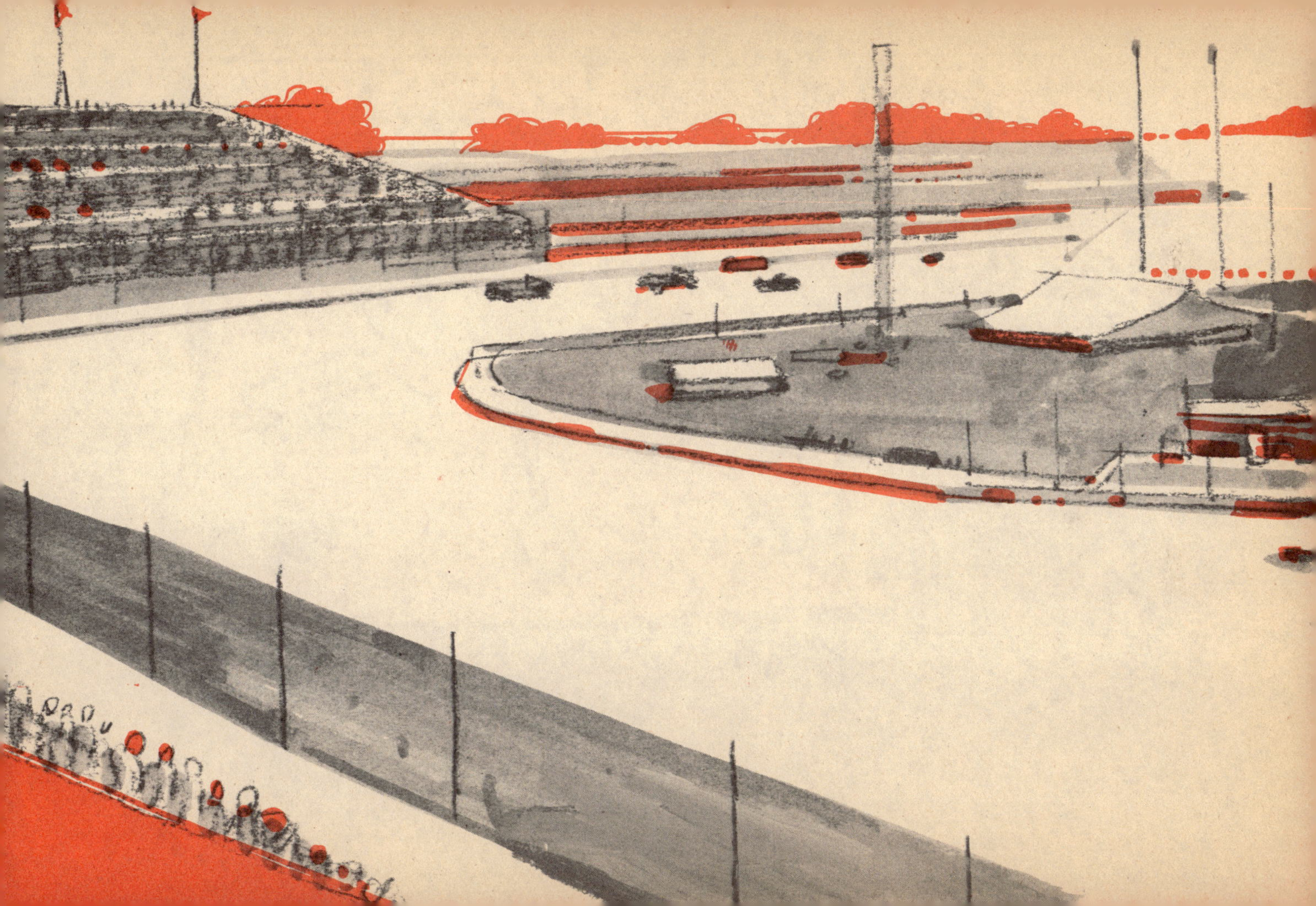

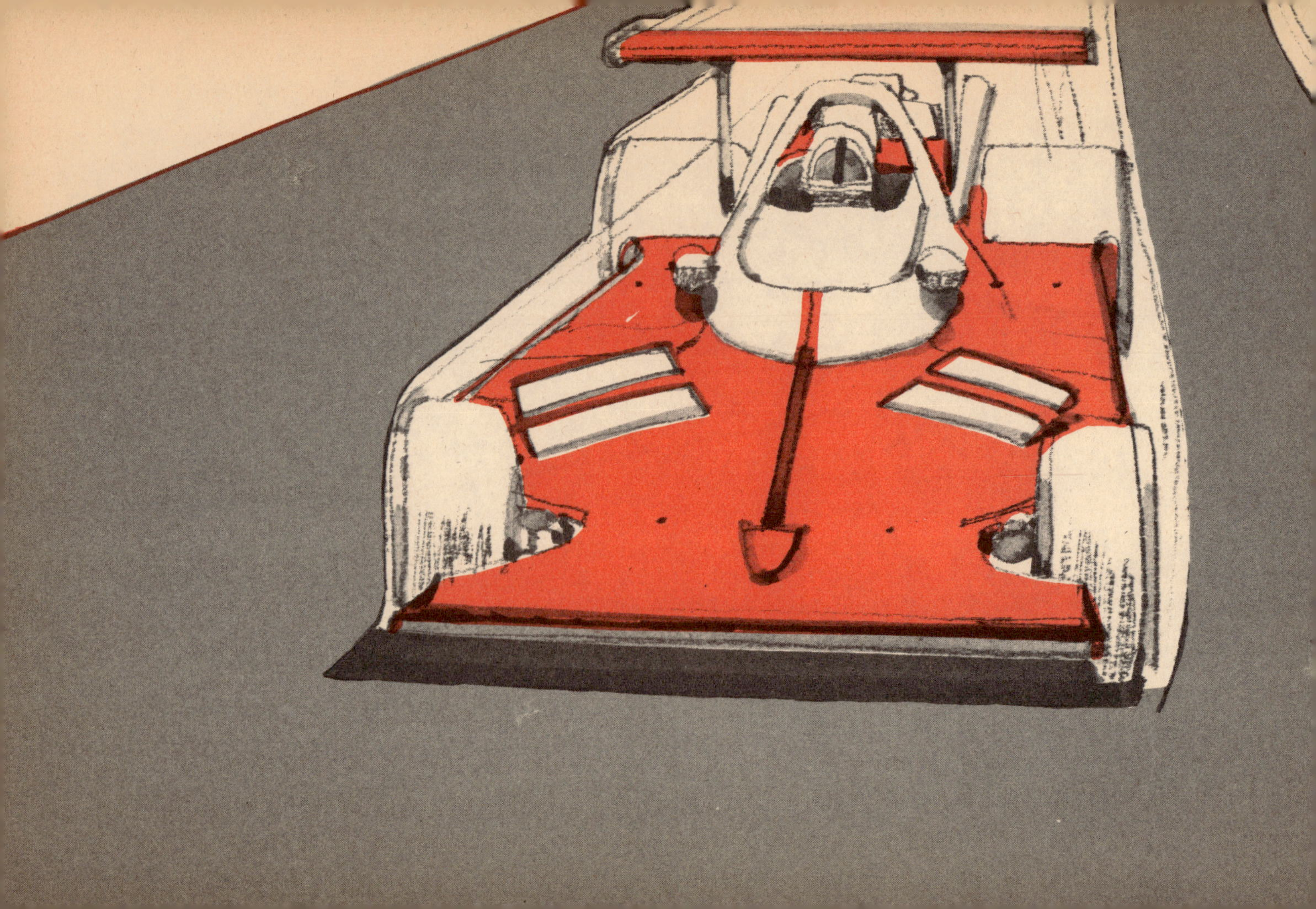

The winner at Indy is the first to finish 200 laps around the track—or 500 miles. That's 805 kilometers!

Before drivers race in the
Indy 500, they must make test drives.
These tests, called trials, are held on
the two weekends before the big race.
The driver with the fastest
time in the trials gets
the best starting
spot in the 500.

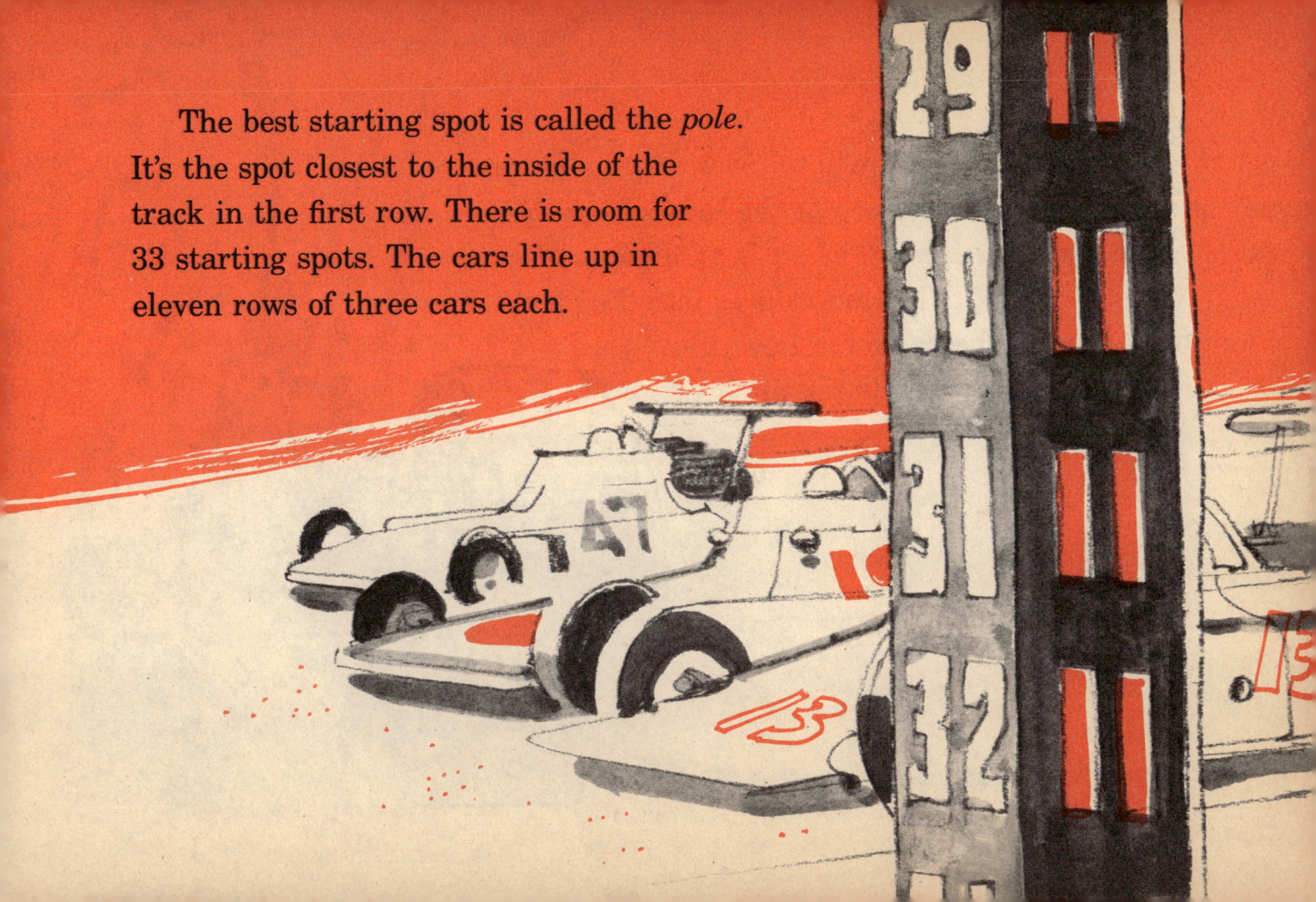

The best starting spot is called the *pole*. It's the spot closest to the inside of the track in the first row. There is room for 33 starting spots. The cars line up in eleven rows of three cars each.

Any racing driver will tell you that no big race is won alone. Races such as the Indy 500 are very often won in the pits. The pit is an area at the side of the track. The driver goes into the pit when the car needs fuel or new tires or repairs. Driving into the pit is called a *pit stop*.

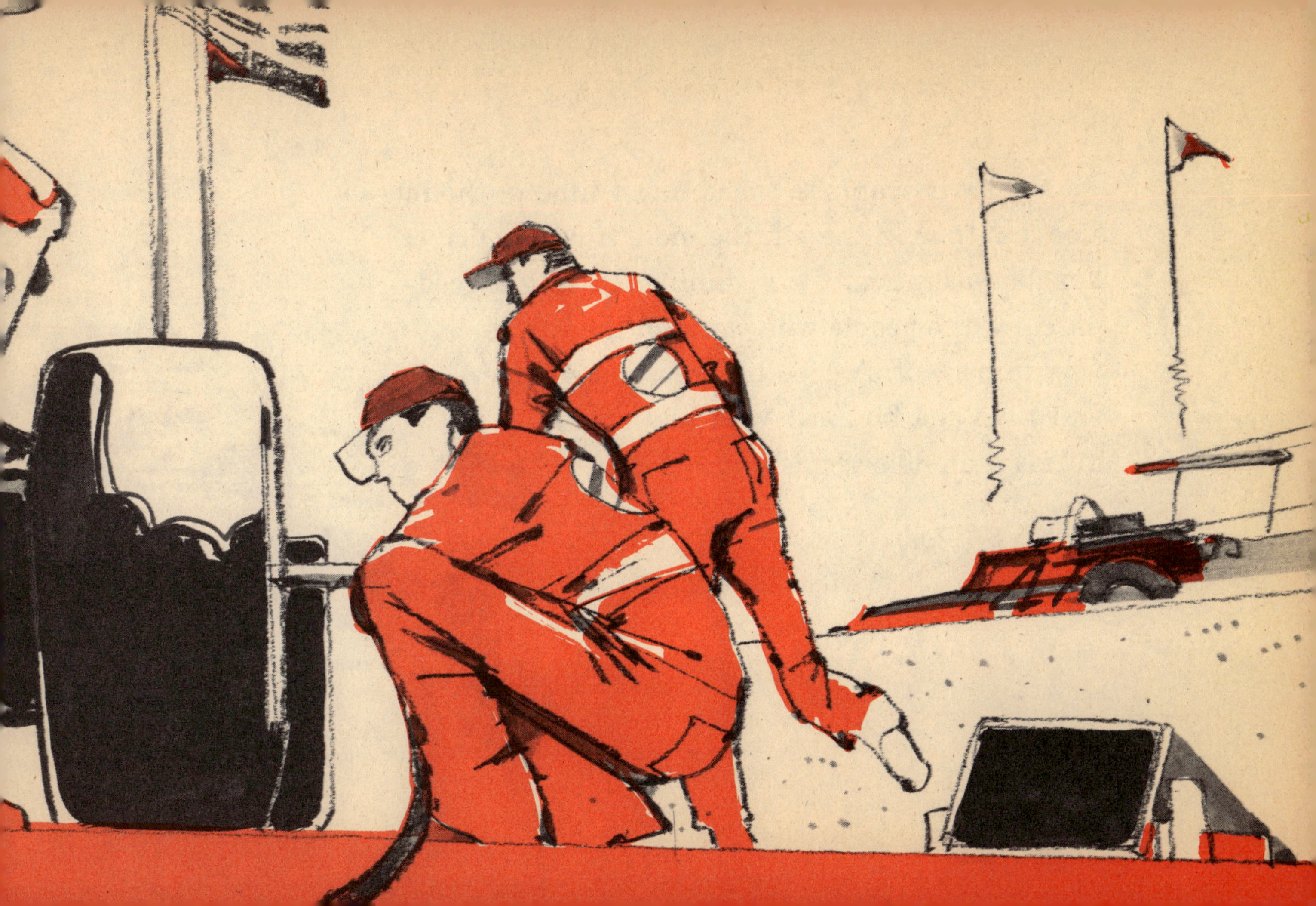

No driver wants to spend much time in the pit. The less time in the pit, the more time the driver has for racing...and for winning. Having a good pit crew, the people who work on the car, is very important. A good pit crew can change four tires and fill a car with fuel in less than 30 seconds!

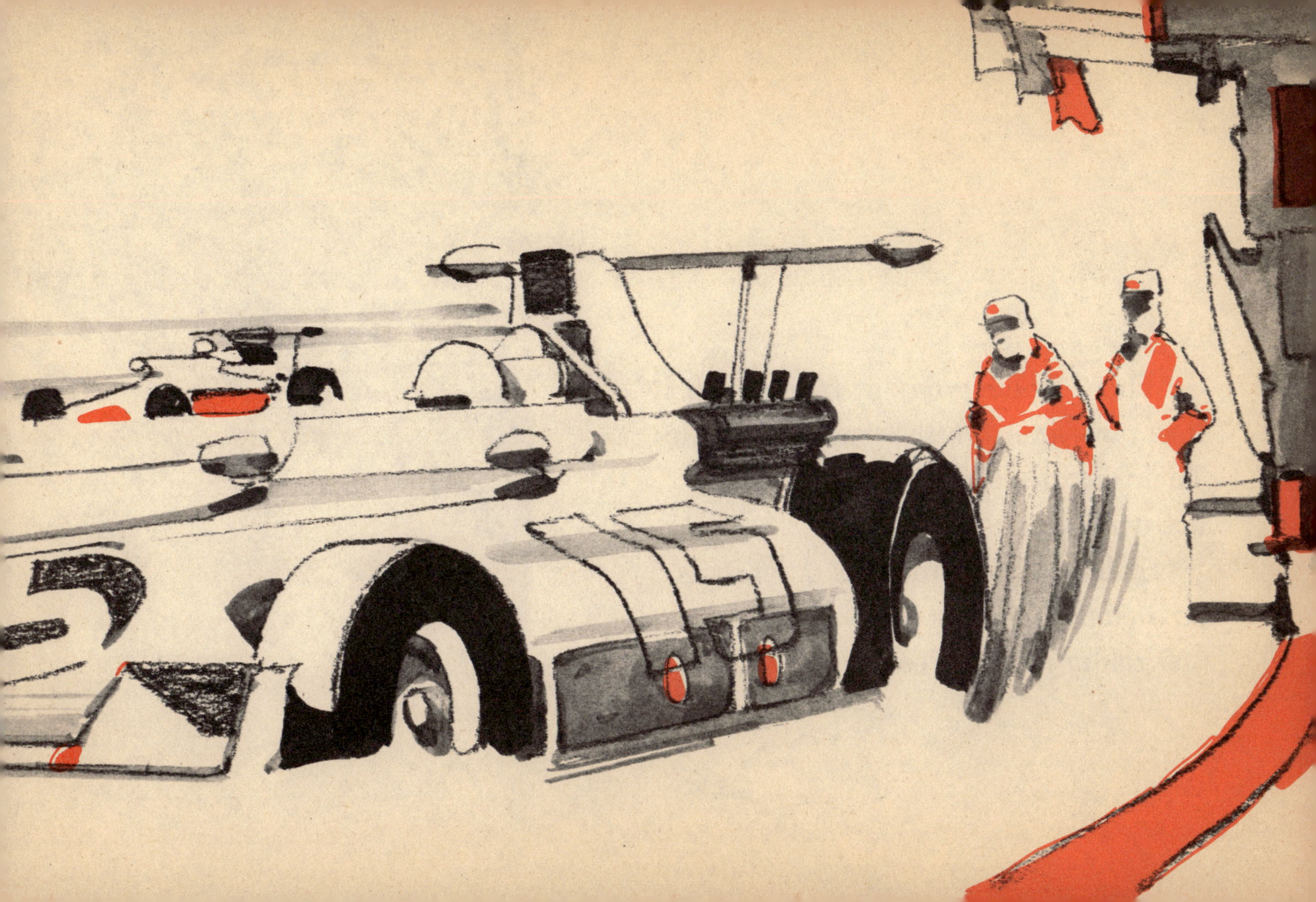

This is the big day at Indianapolis! It is race time. On the track sit 33 cars. Their engines are still, their drivers are waiting.

Suddenly everything is quiet. It is as though 300,000 people and 33 drivers are holding their breath.

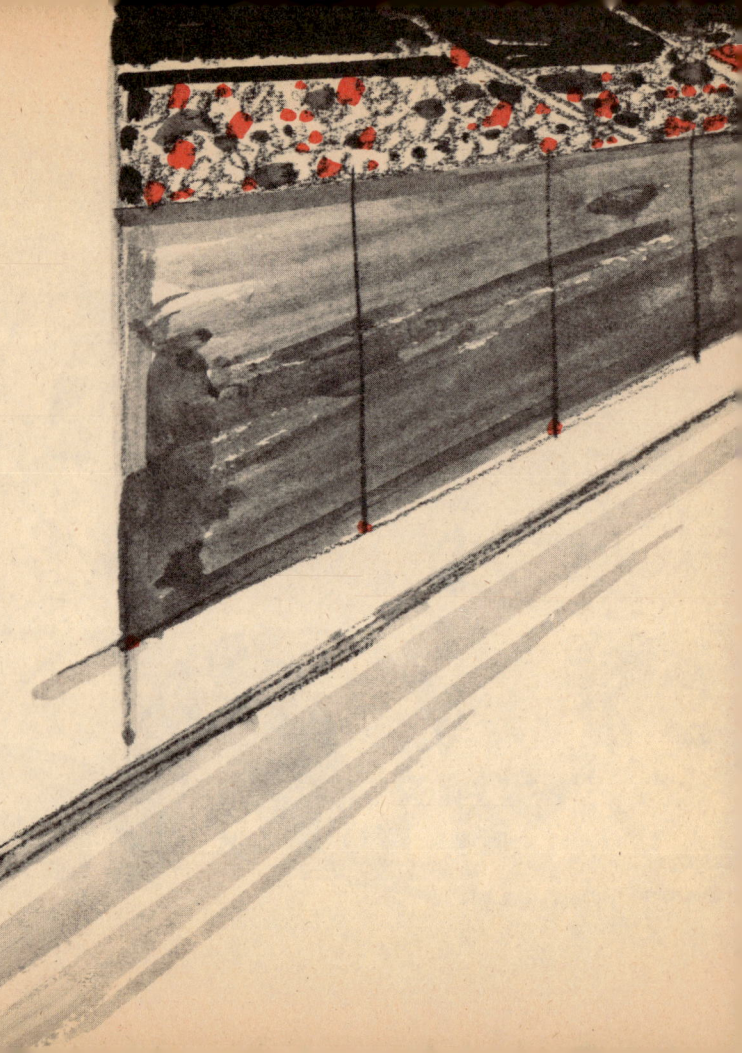

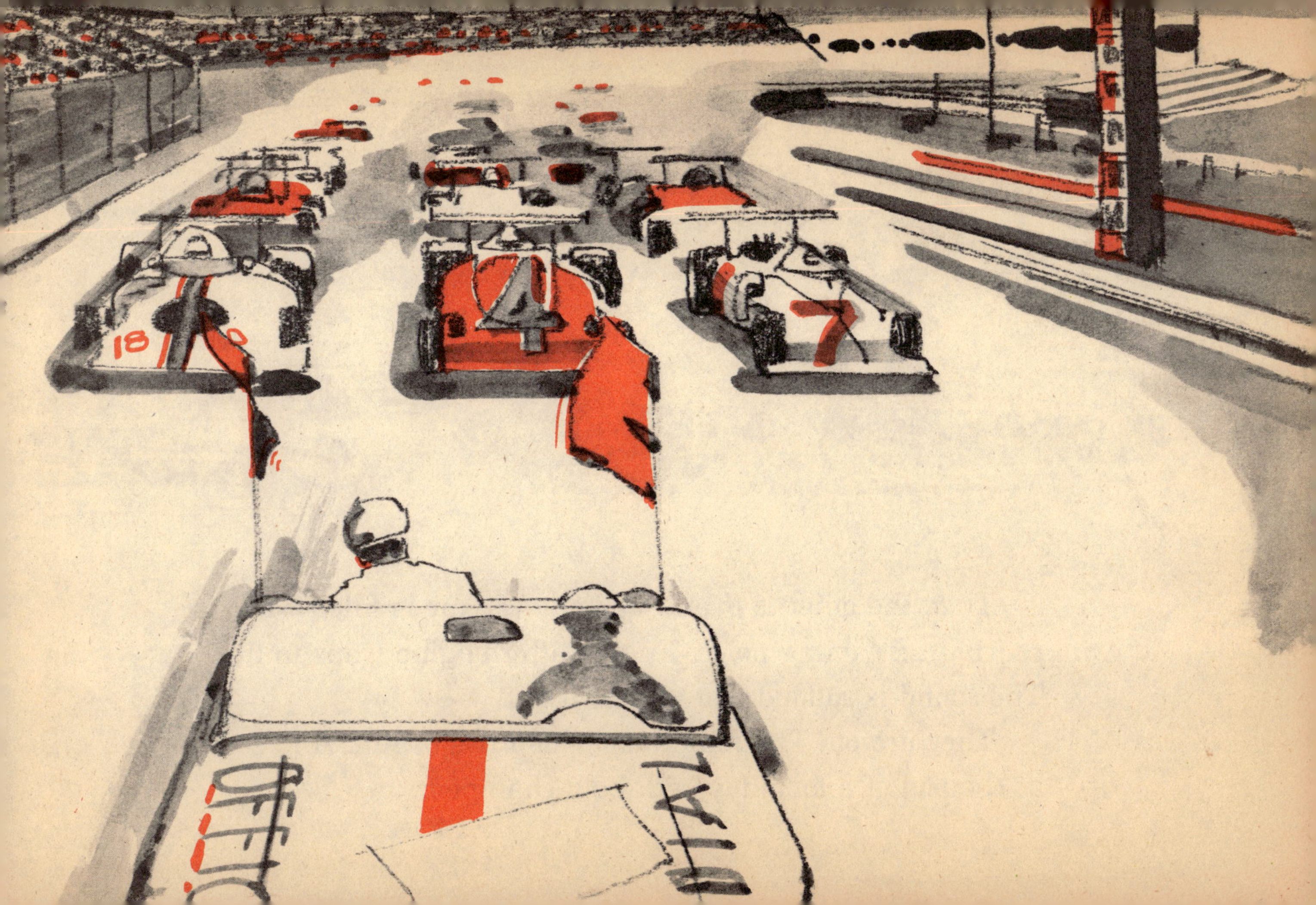
18
4
7

Then the quiet is over. Suddenly the air is filled with roaring, screaming noise. Engine after engine leaps to life. The sound is so loud you cannot think.

They are off! The Indianapolis 500 has begun. And someone, at the end of a long day, will be a champion.